AT ALL
COSTS

THE RED ZONE

AT ALL COSTS

PATRICK JONES AND BRENT CHARTIER

darbycreek

MINNEAPOLIS

Darby Creek
A division of Lerner Publishing Group, Inc.
241 First Avenue North
Minneapolis, MN 55401 USA

For reading levels and more information, look up this title at www.lernerbooks.com.

The images in this book are used with the permission of: © Mike Powell/ CORBIS © iStockphoto.com/mack2happy (grass turf).

Main body text set in Janson Text LT Std 12/17.5.
Typeface provided by Linotype AG.

Library of Congress Cataloging-in-Publication Data

Jones, Patrick, 1961–
        At all costs / by Patrick Jones and Brent Chartier.
            pages   cm. — (The red zone ; #4)
        Summary: "Kyle doesn't see much game time. Mike is more successful—even if he's taken some hits. When Kyle realizes a hole in the concussion detection program, he has to decide whether to tell his friend"— Provided by publisher.
        ISBN 978–1–4677–2129–5 (lib. bdg. : alk. paper)
        ISBN 978–1–4677–4652–6 (eBook)
        [1. Football—Fiction. 2. Best friends—Fiction 3. Friendship—Fiction. 4. High schools—Fiction. 5. Schools—Fiction. 6. Brain—Concussion—Fiction. 7. Conduct of life—Fiction.] I. Chartier, Brent. II. Title.
PZ7.J7242At 2014
[Fic]—dc23   2013041072

Manufactured in the United States of America
1 – SB – 7/15/14

TO CASEY—NO FATHER
LOVES A SON MORE.
—BC

PROLOGUE / TUESDAY, OCTOBER 1— E-MAIL TO COACH ZACHARY FROM THE SCHOOL BOARD PRESIDENT

Coach Zachary:

The Troy School Board thanks you—again— for an exciting football season. It looks as though the team may make it to the playoffs, which benefits the school far beyond what happens on the field.

The purpose of my e-mail is to formally introduce you to a program the school board voted upon last month. We'll be working with Ohio State University to study new ways to identify concussions among student athletes, including boys' football, hockey, wrestling, soccer, and the girls' cheerleading and soccer squads. I've cc'd our contact at State, Dr. Larry Nussbaum, on this message. I trust you'll contact Dr. Nussbaum to discuss the program and how best to introduce it to student athletes and their parents.

Reach me should you have any questions.

Carol Finley

President, Troy School Board

Slam!

Someone's going to get hurt.

Screech!

Someone should say something.

Zeke "Z-Man" Muller and my best buddy, Mike Miller, race to the back, where a circle of desks has been cleared. Everyone watches as the two guys hunch over in a face-off, their arms outstretched, feet apart—perfect wrestling stances. Last year, Mike beat Zeke for the varsity heavyweight spot. We call Monday practices Film Day, but we might as well call them Mike-and-Zeke-Wrestle Day. These matches give Zeke the chance to get back at Mike. The Troy Central football team—fifty guys in all— is crowded into this classroom to watch.

Someone counts down to zero, and like rams butting heads in the wild, Mike and Zeke slam together, wrapping their arms around each other's necks.

"Take 'em down, Mighty Mike!" I shout.

Zeke brings Mike to the floor with a perfect double-leg takedown and hangs on so he lands on top. Shane Hunter, the Troy Central quarterback, takes center stage, shouting "One! Two!" but in a blink, Mike breaks free, wraps up Zeke's arms, and brings him down for a lightning-fast pin.

I muscle my way through my teammates, just like I push back defensive linemen on the field.

"That's a pin!" I say. "The winner and still champ, Mighty Mike Miller!"

Everyone cheers. Well, everyone except Zeke. Mike jumps up and does a little dance, which is awful to look at because he's such a big guy.

Zeke is still on the floor. "Yeah, well, at least I know what a whistle means," he squeaks.

"He got you, Mike!" Devon Shaw, the team's starting halfback, shouts.

"You deserved that one," adds Terry Foster, another starting back. Just like on the field, big guys like me take the hits, but the Big Six backs get all the attention. It's not fair, but what is?

Zeke's referring to the first play of last Friday's game. On the opening kickoff, the super-speedy Orlando returned the ball twenty-two yards before being slammed to the ground. The whistle blew, signaling the end of the play. But Mike, who only started on special teams this year, steamrolled an opposing player to the grass, drawing the penalty—unsportsmanlike conduct for a late hit. *What goes around . . .*, I thought. In the game before, Mike himself had been destroyed by a late hit near the end of the game.

Mike laughs off Zeke's comment and takes a seat at the desk next to mine, just as he's done every day since our first practice freshman year. The rest of the team sits and waits for Coach.

"I'm gonna hear about that play for a while, aren't I, Kyle?" Mike asks me.

"Only as long as your ears work," I say. "You gotta use your head on the field. Remember, there are two lockers at State with our names on them. You and I play smart this season, we get scholarships, and this time next year, we're playing in OSU's stadium to a hundred thousand plus."

"I like that. Two lockers at State," Mike says, smiling.

Ever since we played together on a Troy, Ohio, parks-and-rec midget league ten years ago, Mike and me have shared the same dream—playing football for Ohio State. Now, in our senior year, our dream is within reach, but only if Mike plays his way back to a starting role. He had tried out for tight end but lost the job to a junior, Brian Norwood. Brian lasted a few games, but Mike couldn't earn back his minutes. I knew if determination alone mattered, Mike could start at any position. Ever since the first down of the first practice, he took hit after hit and got back up. But football takes more than guts—it takes brawn *and* brain.

"Look, Mike, I'm trying to get Coach Whitson to give you another chance at tight end, but—"

At that moment, Coach Zachary and his assistants—eight in all—enter the room.

"Before we start game films, I'm passing out a letter to give to your parents," Coach says as his assistants spread out across the room. "This Wednesday night, we're holding a mandatory meeting for parents and players. You're gonna be guinea pigs. The university wants to test everyone for concussions."

Mike leans over. "I don't want anyone studying my brain," he murmurs.

I whisper back, "Because if they x-rayed your head, they wouldn't find anything, right?" But Mike doesn't laugh.

Then Coach Zachary turns on the film, and there it is: the kickoff, Mike throwing a vicious block, Orlando scrambling, the whistle, and then Mike's second hit, running over a lineman like an out-of-control train.

Coach pauses the film after Mike draws the penalty. "Mr. Miller," he says.

"Yes, sir!" Mike shouts back.

"Mr. Miller, do you know what a whistle means?" The room explodes as everyone—from the coaches through the starting backs down to the scrubs and even Mike—laughs. Everyone but me.

2 / TUESDAY, OCTOBER 15— HISTORY CLASS

Mike trudges in and drops his books on the table with a thump. He's brought more than the book for history class. He brought his whole locker.

"Why do you bring all of your books to every class?" I ask.

"Keeps me conditioned," he says, showing off his biceps. "Every moment of every day is an opportunity to be a better football player. Call it strength training."

Ms. Bartlett takes roll, then we break into small groups for our project—a class presentation on a major battle from the American Civil War. In the group, it's me; Mike; my girlfriend, Tammy; and Rashad, the class brain. Rashad says he's been watching the History Channel since he was in a crib. Given that history is the furthest thing from our minds during football season, we welcomed him to our group with open arms.

Across the room is Cindy, a new girl and Tammy's new best friend. And, according to Tammy, she's got a crush on Mighty Mike.

Rashad speaks first. "Did everyone do their research on Sherman's March?"

Tammy sets a few pages in front of him, then goes back to holding my hand.

Mike and I look at each other. "We've been too busy with practice," I say.

"And partying? You hung over or what?" Rashad asks Mike, who, for whatever reason, wears sunglasses. Mike used to party with the backs, but now that he's not a starter, he's exiled from the Big Six.

Tammy slaps my arm. "You've had a week to do research. Come on, guys!" she says.

"But it's foot—" I start when Mike takes over.

"Research?" asks Mike. "You want research? Get a load of this." He reaches into his pocket and pulls out a rusted ball no bigger than a golf ball. He sets it on the table in front of Rashad with a thud.

"Civil War era. Iron. Small-bore cannon shot," Rashad says as he examines it.

"All true," Mike says. "My uncle found it when he was stationed at Hunter Army Airfield in Georgia. He says it could've come from one of Sherman's own cannons."

Tammy and I are impressed, but Rashad is flush with excitement, as though every cheerleader in the school just asked him to this weekend's homecoming dance.

"Rashad, I am prepared, my man," Mike says. But Rashad is gone. He's rushed over to a class computer, which leaves the three of us to talk about what really matters—homecoming.

"You haven't asked her yet?" shouts Tammy.

Mike has yet to approach Cindy. Tammy says he just has to say the words. "How hard is that?" she asks.

"I'll get around to it—there's time," replies Mike.

"Like, four days," I say.

"Kyle, it's not like we haven't been busy. Besides, I asked for the night off from Gus's. That's a start." Mike's referring to Gus's Diner, where he works part-time to help his family pay bills.

Tammy takes a stand. "You don't ask her by the end of the day, I will never, *ever* help you with your science homework again."

Mike blushes and rubs the back of his head.

"So cool!" Rashad says. He's pointing at the computer screen, holding the ball, and speaking excitedly to Ms. Bartlett at the same time.

"By the way," I ask. "Is that thing really from the Civil War?"

Mike grins. "Sure enough. My uncle's a Civil War reenactor. He has dozens of them."

"I never understood why people would want

to play make-believe war," says Tammy. "All the bodies laid out on the field."

I offer up a high five to Mike. "Sounds a lot like Troy Central football!" I say as our hands slap. The smack echoes through the room like one of Sherman's cannon shots.

3 / TUESDAY, OCTOBER 15—
AFTERNOON PRACTICE

"That's the biggest flamingo I've ever seen!" Shane cracks. Everybody laughs—not so much at Shane but at the sight of Mike wearing a pink jersey designed for this most public punishment. He stands only on his right leg as Coach Whitson begins to speak.

"As Mr. Miller has two left feet, maybe this will help him lose one of them," Whitson announces. In the practice play before, Mike fell while running a tight-end pass pattern.

Truman Jackson whispers, "What happened to him?" Truman plays left guard next to me.

"What do you mean?" I whisper back.

"He used to be good but, man, this year, Mike sucks."

I start to think of excuses, but instead, I fall back into formation. Mike hasn't lost his step or strength, but since losing his starting job, he has lost his confidence. You can see it in his eyes.

Shane calls the play—a sweep with pass option—and we head to the line. I glare at Reggie Edwards, the opposing lineman. We're lab partners in science, putting our brains together. Out here, we smack helmets.

Reggie tries to muscle me, but it doesn't work. I trounce him like Sherman did the rebels. When the whistle blows seconds later, rather than let Devon run, Shane elects to pass—unsuccessfully—and I offer my hand to Reggie. "Thanks." He grabs my hand, squeezes it hard, and slaps me on the back.

"When you two ladies are done holding

hands, maybe we can play football!" Coach Colby shouts.

More laughter. It's a Troy football rule: laugh at every coach's joke, even if it is stupid.

We finish the scrimmage with a touchdown. Troy football is built on offense, and I more than do my part. My name will never run in the papers, but I make the backs look good. When you're on the line, that's your job: cover for others at all costs.

"Flamingo, let's see you run sprints!" Coach Whitson yells.

Mike puts his leg down and races over to me.

Those of us playing remove our helmets and join the scrubs at the forty-yard line, where the "north and south" sprints start. Forty to forty, thirty to thirty, and so on. By goal line to goal line, even Devon and Orlando are panting. I'm breathing heavy, but Mike's heaving like he's about to throw up.

"You OK?" I ask.

"Bad lunch."

"So you ate at Gus's?"

Mike doesn't react.

"Grab some grass," Coach Z says. "Except you, Miller. Back on one leg."

The rest of us sit on the field.

Coach continues. "Remember, Wednesday night is this university thing. It is mandatory for you and your parents."

I grumble. My folks don't love football as much as I do, but they'll show up if only to complain. Mike's folks both work nights. One will need to take the night off to attend.

"And here's a little extra wrinkle." Coach Z paces back and forth like a general addressing the troops. "Turns out they want to start testing ASAP, which stands for 'as soon as possible,' geniuses."

Coach Z keeps talking, we keep grumbling, and Mike keeps standing until Coach Whitson tells him to stop. Mike celebrates being back on two feet by throwing up on the field.

4 / WEDNESDAY, OCTOBER 16— HISTORY CLASS

I slip Mike the piece of paper just as the second bell rings.

"Thanks, Kyle."

"No problem," I say.

Mike offers me a ten-dollar bill, but I wave it away. Between football, school, and work at Gus's, Mike has fallen behind, so I did his math homework. He'd do the same for me.

"You don't want anything?" he asks.

"OK, two things. One of those," I say, pointing to the energy drink in Mike's hand.

He quickly pops two white pills into his mouth—Mrs. Bartlett doesn't see, as she's distracted by Rashad's antics—and gulps it down.

"Sorry, bro, that was my last one. So what's the other thing?" he asks, adjusting his shades.

"Ask Cindy to homecoming already," Tammy answers for me.

Mike says nothing. Instead, he rubs the back of his neck.

"You OK?" I ask, but there's no answer.

Mrs. Bartlett turns off the lights, and Mike removes his shades. The PowerPoint shows more Civil War photos—conquering heroes, dead bodies, burned buildings.

"So, Mr. Miller, what was the key to Sherman's victory?" Mrs. Bartlett asks.

There's silence, followed by snickers. I glance at Mike whose head is on the desk, his eyes closed.

"*Mike*," I hiss.

Mrs. Bartlett's turns on the light and calls his name again. His head pops up, and the shades go on. She repeats the question, and Mike stumbles for an answer. I jump in and rescue Mike with facts and figures.

"In your small groups, see if you can expand upon Mike and Kyle's answer," Mrs. Bartlett says as she frowns at Mike.

Desks turn, but not Mike's. Instead, he heads straight to a classroom computer.

"What's with him?" Tammy asks.

I shrug and leave her and Rashad as I follow Mike to the computer.

"You OK?" I ask. "Maybe no one else notices, but I can tell something's wrong."

He looks over my shoulder to see if anyone else can hear. "Kyle, I can trust you, right?"

I lean in and give Mike my look of deep concern.

"Last week, when I drew that penalty, I think I got my bell rung right after the kick-off. I mean, you know me, Kyle. I play hard, but I play by the rules." We both ignore the math homework I did for him. "I swear I didn't hear the whistle. It's like those ten seconds of my life are just missing."

"Could it have been an alien abduction?" I say, but again Mike doesn't laugh. He keeps rubbing the back of his head.

"I think I got concussed, but I can't tell Coach, 'cause he won't play me, especially now with these brain guys coming. And if I don't get my minutes, I don't get a scholarship, and we don't go to State together. It sucks."

I push my way toward the computer and bring up the Wikipedia entry on *concussion*.

"Search again," says Mike. "Any idiot can post something on Wikipedia." Mike laughs at his own joke—we created fake Wikipedia pages for all of our coaches over the summer. Mike thinks the coaches found out and *that's* why he's not playing.

He takes the keyboard and finds the Cleveland Clinic website. Together, we read the list of concussion symptoms: headache, nausea, hearing problems, light or noise sensitivity.

"Kyle, I got all this," Mike whispers, pointing to the screen, "and with that test Coach says we all—"

"Wait, how do you take a test?" I ask. "You study for it, right?"

I take back the keyboard and search for con-cussion tests and Ohio State University. We read silently how the test is likely to work—an eye exam followed by a written test and then something called diffusion tensor imaging for a player suspected of having a concussion.

"I'm worried, Kyle. I mean, this could be it—the end of everything." There's a tremor in his voice. If I could see his eyes under the shades, I might see a tear or at least a look of fear.

"Look, tonight is just a meeting. They won't test us," I say. "I bet by the time the test comes up, you'll be fine."

Kyle takes a deep breath. "And if I'm not?"

I place a hand on his shoulder. "Look, I got this, bro."

On the keyboard, I add three words to the "concussion test" search: *how to beat.*

5 / WEDNESDAY, OCTOBER 16— CONCUSSION PROGRAM MEETING

The bleachers and folding chairs on the gym floor are nearly packed at the start of the meeting. School board members sit before the crowd, talking and laughing. Next to them, a man and a woman in red-and-white OSU polos stand and scan the crowd. Beside them is this huge guy, staring off into space. Coach Zachary is parked to the side, almost sneering at these invaders to his turf.

I file in with the team, Mike next to me as always.

"Kyle! Over here!" It's my mother, sitting in the bleachers. Dad's next to her, his arms folded across his chest. I just know he hates being here, seeing as he's just put in ten hours at the factory.

"I gotta sit with the team," I say, waving, although it's not true.

"OK," she says.

Mike bumps my arm. "I give up," he tells me. "I can't go through with this. I'm telling coach."

I grab his arm. "No, you're not. We can do this."

We find chairs in back, and after a welcome speech from the board president, one of the polo shirts steps forward.

"Thank you for coming. I'm Dr. Nussbaum, with Ohio State's Sports Injury Center. I'm here to tell you about our program, Brain CRIP, which stands for Brain Concussion Recognition and Intervention Program."

Five minutes into the program, someone raises a hand. "My son has a doctor. Won't his doctor tell me if something's wrong?" I recognize the man as Shane's father. Like his son, he's got to be the center of attention.

Next is Brian Norwood's dad, a big Trojan High football booster. "My son's played football twelve years, and he's never had a problem. Why do this now?"

"Yeah, it's not like pro football," says Dylan's father. "If you guys find something, he could lose out on scholarships, and that's the only way he's gonna make it to college."

If Mike's dad were here, I'm sure he'd say the same thing, except he couldn't get the night off. He's always working. His mom too.

There's murmuring throughout the gym, and Nussbaum gives a look like he's stumbled upon a tribe of headhunters. The board president sits stone-faced, pretending not to notice.

The woman who came with the doctor steps up. "Folks, please," she says. When everyone's quiet, she continues. "My name is Sue Winters. I'm a nurse, working with Dr. Nussbaum on Brain CRIP. No, this isn't pro football. And while scholarships may be at risk, something even more important is as well—your sons' future. Young people have the highest risk for concussion. We're not talking about head colds or beestings. This is the most serious, preventable threat to a young athlete's future. Let me show you."

With that, she motions to the huge guy who stands and slowly steps up to join the researchers, his left leg dragging on the floor.

Dr. Nussbaum takes over. "This is Stuart. He's a junior at Ohio State. This summer, he experienced a concussion while playing street hockey on campus. He fell headfirst into a parked car with about the same amount of force as helmet-to-helmet contact in football. Stuart will never regain complete use of his left side. And he's twenty."

I look over as Mike pops more aspirin.

"You'll be fine," I whisper.

"I hope you're right."

Nussbaum continues his talk. We learn that football players will be tested Friday.

I watch Mike rub his forehead. I think about what he said. I hope I'm right too.

6 / THURSDAY, OCTOBER 17—
AFTER FOOTBALL PRACTICE

"Oh, garçon!" I snap my fingers, which creates the expected sigh from Tammy.

"Don't embarrass him!" she says.

We're at Gus's Diner, enjoying two large cokes, two plates of fries, and one side of trying to crack Mike up.

"But he's my best friend," I say. "That's what we do."

Mike shows up with a big smile and no

shades, even under the bright lights of Gus's.

"Can I help you?" Mike asks.

Tammy starts in about Cindy. "If you don't ask her out, I'm doing it for you. I mean you're almost eighteen, old enough to join the army, but you're too scared to ask—"

"Look, I'll do it," Mike snaps.

"*Sor*-ry." Tammy stretches out the word to last a minute. "What's with you, anyway?"

"Nothing."

That's far from the truth, but Tammy doesn't know it—and she doesn't need to know, either. She'd be happier if I never picked up a football—she's afraid I'll get hurt. She'd hate to hear about Mike's injury, but she also hates it when I keep secrets from her. I'm torn.

"She's kidding," I say to Mike. "Right, Tammy?" I squeeze her hand gently.

"Maybe." Tammy crosses her arms.

"What if she says no?" Mike asks Tammy. He doesn't need another hit to his ego, for sure.

"She won't. Trust me."

"Mike!" Gus yells from the register. Mike scampers away from the table.

I turn back to Tammy, but she's on the phone.

"So you *would* go to homecoming with him, right?" Tammy says. She sets the phone down and puts it on speaker.

"Sure, but what's taking him so long?" Cindy asks.

"He's just shy," Tammy answers.

"For a guy who struts around with sunglasses, he doesn't act shy."

"Mike's a man of action, not words!" I say into the phone.

"Am I on speaker?" Cindy shouts.

Tammy picks up the phone, and as she and Cindy talk more, I leave the table to find Mike and share the good news. I glance around the restaurant, but he's nowhere in sight. I text him, but he doesn't reply. Since Tammy's still on the phone, I step outside and glance around the parking lot. I see Mike's car, so he must be nearby.

I text him again. Still nothing. I check the time and figure I'd better get home—I have my homework, Mike's homework, and new plays in the playbook to study. I grab a pen from my jacket and pull out the receipt for the flowers I bought Tammy for homecoming. *Call Cindy, now. Touchdown guaranteed*, I write.

I lift the wiper blade of his car and put the note underneath it, but as I'm about to leave, I hear something from inside the car. I look inside to see Mike, lying across the backseat. I pound on the door. He rolls over, sits up, and opens the door.

"You OK?" I ask.

He doesn't answer, just rubs his forehead.

"Look, I got the concussion test figured out. Really researched the way they look for symptoms," I say. "That'll be one less thing you can stress over."

"How?" Mike asks.

"That's for me to know and you to find out."

"I'd feel better knowing." His eyes look glazed.

"Trust me," I say.

"I better get back to work."

With that, Mike steps out of the car. I close the door behind him, and he winces.

7 / FRIDAY, OCTOBER 18— TROY CENTRAL HIGH SCHOOL

Troy Central's morning announcements request that football players report to the hallway outside the gym by 11 a.m. By 10:50, I'm in the hallway with Mike, Brian, and Shane.

"They look in my brain, all they'll see is Jenny, Jenny, Jenny," says Shane, referring to his current girlfriend—I think. He's had so many, no one could keep count.

"That's funny," says Mike. "She's been in

my brain all morning too."

Shane grins and throws a book at Mike. It's the old Mike—big, fun, and rude.

Mike snatches the book and holds it high, like he's just caught a pass.

"Mr. Hunter!" booms Coach Zachary, who's a few steps behind us.

The four of us stop and turn.

Shane stiffens. "Yes, sir."

"Watch that arm," Coach says. "You'll need it for tonight against the Highlanders."

Shane radiates such smugness that even compliments bounce off him, but Coach doesn't notice, just like he doesn't notice or speak to the rest of us.

"Sure thing, Coach," Shane says.

"And Mike, nice catch. Hope you still got it tonight. I'm starting you at tight end," Coach says.

This is great news—but Mike has to pass the concussion test first.

In the hallway outside the gym, players stand in line against the wall while Dr. Nussbaum speaks. "This is a simple ocular exam," he says. I'm going to look into your eyes with this pen-light. When you finish here, report to room 108 for the written portion." He looks over at Mike. "And since this is an eye exam, I'll need you to remove your sunglasses."

Mike shoves the glasses into his pocket as we watch Nussbaum shine his light into the eyes of player after player. The test takes all of twenty seconds, so the line goes fast.

I get behind Mike. "Here, you go ahead of me," I say.

"No problem," says Mike.

Mike's spirits are up, which is a good thing.

When it's Mike's turn, Nussbaum shines his light. "OK, look up ... look right ... hmmmm ... look   left ... hmmmm ... look right again ... look down—"

Based on what we learned about beating the test, Mike agreed to lie to the doctor, but waiting for him to speak, I can't stand the suspense.

"Dr. Nussbaum, he's got a really bad head cold," I say. "Think that might be a problem?"

Nussbaum gives me a look like I just interrupted his phone call with the president. "Sinusitis?" he asks Mike.

Mike shrugs. "Sure," he says. "I mean, yes."

"Take care of that," Nussbaum tells Mike. "Next."

One test down, one to go.

In the classroom, I recognize Nurse Winters from the parent meeting. Every desk has a big folder and a pencil on it. I take a seat next to Mike—of course.

When all players are in the room, Winters speaks. "This is a timed test. Fifteen minutes," she says. "But relax. You won't be graded. When I say 'go,' open the envelope, put your name on the test, and begin."

She steps back to the desk and turns on a timer. "Go."

I open the envelope. Just as Mike and I had expected after we visited the Ohio State website, the test is part connect-the-dots, part math, part spelling, and all easy. There's a part where I have to draw what looks like a smiley face in the middle of a sailboat. I save it for last.

I look at Mike who's squinting and using more eraser than lead.

"Time's up," says the woman after the timer dings. No duh.

She collects the tests, and everyone starts piling out of the room except Mike, Zeke, and me.

I go to the desk while Mike stands in the door. Zeke is about to become an unwilling accomplice.

On cue, Mike shouts "What's your problem, Zeke?" as Zeke approaches the door. "You have something to say to me?"

Zeke's wearing his usual stunned look. "Out of my way, man."

"Make me!" Mike says.

Zeke decides he will, and it's on as the two push, shove, and shout their way into the hall. Immediately, the nurse rushes toward them—as though there's anything she can do to stop these behemoths—leaving the tests on the desk.

I pounce on the tests like a fumble and flip

through the pile, searching for Mike's test. It's not hard to find—it's as messy as cafeteria food.

As Mike and Zeke yell and push, I change six answers, finish Mike's sailboat drawing, and cross my fingers that it's smooth sailing for the rest of the season.

8 / FRIDAY, OCTOBER 18—
HOME GAME AGAINST THE OAK HILLS
HIGHLANDERS

I closed my eyes, and I saw it: the perfect block. Shane would take the snap and either pitch to Devon, hand off to Dylan, or take off with it himself. Opposing linemen would rush, but I'd knock them out of the way while Shane or one of the backs sprinted toward daylight. I was a bulldozer for backfield freedom.

Dressed up, sitting on the bench in the

locker room, I saw the game in my head, every split-second battle before it happened. I almost hated to actually play the game and surrender the beauty of my smooth dream for gritty reality.

"Listen up!" Coach Zachary shouts. In a split second, every conversation stops. "I have the results of the concussion tests."

The silence holds sway over the room.

"The doctor says you're all head cases, but it's not like I didn't know that all along," Coach says and then laughs. "You all passed and are cleared to play."

"Cleared to win!" shouts Mike.

Other players chime in. "We're climbing Oak Hill and taking the Highlanders down!" Brian shouts.

Coach is normally controlled, but every now and then, he lets everyone holler what they feel. And sometimes I did, but not tonight. I want to win, but my thoughts are a coin flip. Tails? Mike sits. Heads? Mike plays and excels. I can't bring myself to think about a third option: Mike plays and gets hurt again.

Coach keeps talking, but I don't focus until his last words: "We take the Highlanders, and we're one game closer to meeting—and beating—Athens!"

The D-end for the Highlanders moves like a snowplow—strong but slow. By the third quarter, I find myself almost feeling sorry for him. He picks himself off the ground again and again as Devon, Dylan, and Shane roar past him.

Highlander's linebackers blitz constantly, never allowing Shane to set up and throw. Since we control the line, Coach Whitson decides to slog out the running game. Every time the play came in—almost always another rush—I thought I could hear Shane's teeth grind. He wanted to run and gun, but Coach knew the enemy. Just like the Union army, we'd win a slow war of attrition.

"Is it a pass?" Shane asks the player, running into the huddle.

"Blue dog, twenty-three," comes the reply—playbook code for a short pass to Mike.

"Yes," says Mike.

With the game in the middle of the field, Coach runs more and more plays with a tight end, so Mike earns his minutes. He catches a few short passes, takes a few hits, but it's his best game yet. With every catch and every yard earned, Mike earns back Coach's trust.

I take my place on the line, wait for the count, and then explode like a cannonball. As the D-end eats turf, I sprint ahead for a second block on an outside linebacker, who I nail hard just as Mike catches the flare pass. He slips a tackle and turns on the speed. His brains might be scrambled, but his legs pump like pistons into the end zone.

Even though Shane swept around the left end for two extra points, I felt cheated with every play that didn't come my way. But a touchdown and the two gave us a sixteen-point lead going into the final quarter.

Fresh from landing a touchdown, Mike races down the field on the kickoff, making a spectacular tackle. But when he comes off the field, I can tell something is wrong. I pull him away from the coaches to the far end of the bench.

"Did I score?" Mike asks as we stand on the sidelines.

"Focus, Mike, focus," I say.

Coach Kramer, leader of special teams, comes over and pats Mike's grass-stained pants. "Great tackle, Miller!"

Mike whispers to me, "What did he say? I didn't hear him." He turns and shouts to Coach K, "Did I score?"

"What?" Coach K asks.

I place myself like a stone wall between Coach K and Mike.

"He wants to know if he scored points with you!" I shout, trying to keep Coach away.

"Did I score?" Mike yells louder, as though he can't hear the sound of his voice.

I turn to Mike. "Here, hold your helmet!" I scream. As he does so, in a furious few seconds, I snap the chin strap off and yank at his right shoulder pad.

"Did I score?" Mike says again. I feel Coach Kramer behind us.

I take one step out of the way. "Look, Coach, his equipment is all messed up."

Kramer surveys the damage I caused.

"I'll help him get cleaned up," I say.

Coach nods.

With that, I grab Mike's arm, and we sprint to the locker room. The ugly gray floor is a welcome sight, if only for a second. Mike uglies it up, covering a small corner with vomit.

9 / FRIDAY, OCTOBER 18— AT GUS'S, AFTER THE GAME

"Why are you pushing this?" I palm two of the diner's salt-and-pepper shakers, then smack them together like a couple of D-lineman. "He barely knows Cindy."

"Because she's my friend," Tammy says with a tone that smacks like a head slap.

"How did *your* friend's homecoming date become *my* problem?" I ask.

"We're a couple, Kyle," Tammy says.

"Couples do things for each other. He has tomorrow night off. What's his problem?"

"Like I said, he barely knows her." Truth is, for all his on-field bravado, Mike is a shy guy. He'd rather slam headfirst into a blitzing linebacker than talk to a girl he barely knows. Last year, when he was one of the Big Six, it wasn't an issue—girls flocked all moth-and-flame-like to the backs. Now that he's become another drone with a number on his jersey, I don't think he can stand another chip at his confidence.

"For you, I'll ask again," I say.

"You didn't answer my question. I asked, what is Mike's problem?" She runs down all of the ways in which Mike has been acting odd over the past few days—since he made that hard tackle on the first kickoff last game. "Where is he anyway?" Tammy asks.

"I'll check," I say calmly, although my heart's beating like it does before a snap. After throwing up in the locker room, Mike returned to play, but Coach Whitson pulled him from the offense after he missed a block and dropped a pass on the same nightmare set of downs.

I rise from the table and kiss Tammy's perfect lips. "I'll be right back," I say as I walk to the bathroom.

The door is locked. "Mike, you in there?" There's no answer. I text him: *Open the door, ask Cindy out.*

There's a faint commotion: running water and the clicking of a lock. "You can come in," Mike says.

He turns and drops to his knees to finish cleaning up the vomit. Like the pass he dropped, he missed the toilet by a few inches.

"Let me help," I say.

"Thanks," he mumbles.

"Mike," I start, "maybe it's time you tell Coach you—"

Mike grabs my wrist and pinches it like a pair of human pliers. "No. I can't."

"But you're hurt?"

"He'd bench me for sure." Mike squeezes my wrist harder. "If I sit on the bench, I don't go to college. If I don't go to college, then what? Stay here and work two crappy jobs like my parents? Is that what you want for me?"

"No," I say quietly.

Mike's made it obvious—I can't say a word to Coach. Not now, not tomorrow, not ever.

"Mike, can I see your phone?" Tammy asks when we return to the table.

Mike hands it over.

Tammy looks at her phone, then dials a number on Mike's. Mike's fuming, but I know he'll do me this favor.

"Hold for Mr. Miller," says Tammy as she hands Mike his phone.

"Hey, Cindy. It's, uh, me, Mike Miller. And I was—"

Mike walks to the front door, so Tammy and I don't get to hear the rest.

"See, how hard was that?" Tammy looks at me so pleased with herself.

"Whatever makes you happy." I kiss her and pull her tight.

"Buuuut you still haven't answered my question. What's wrong with Mike? And don't lie to me, Kyle!"

I can trust Tammy, I decide, so I tell her everything about Mike and the big hit and his problems, leaving out a few of the vomit-laden details. When I'm through explaining everything, we sit in silence for a moment.

"Why are you doing this?" she finally asks as she rests her head on my shoulder.

"Because he's my friend."

10 / SATURDAY, OCTOBER 19— HOMECOMING

As Tammy and I step from my car, I'm feeling like a million dollars in my black shirt and black tie. Tammy looks great in a short red leather jacket, long black dress, and white corsage.

"Let's act like we own the place," I say as we approach the school entrance.

Tammy smiles and squeezes my hand. "Yes. Let's."

The gym is dark and the music loud. We

decide to walk along the walls, looking for Mike and Cindy, but they're nowhere to be found. A dozen students we recognize are standing in one corner, though. When we get there, the Troy Central assistant principal serves us punch.

"Try texting her again," I tell Tammy.

"I've sent her like twenty texts already. She's not answering."

Twenty is about as many times as I've texted Mike, with the same result.

"Maybe he had to work after all," I think aloud.

"Try calling Gus's, then," Tammy says, which isn't a bad idea.

I pull up Mike's work number and make the call.

"Gus's Eatery. Gus speaking," says the voice on the phone.

"Yes, I'm calling to see if Mike Miller is working tonight?" I ask.

"Who's asking?"

"This is Kyle. We play football together."

"Football? Well, yeah, I had to call Mike in because my other busboy was a no-show. But then I had to send Mike home early."

"Mike came in, but you sent him home early?" I repeat the conversation for Tammy.

"Yeah, he was no good to me here. I had to say everything twice, and he was just—I don't know. You ever bus tables? I'll probably have an opening soon." From the tone in Gus's voice, it doesn't sound like he's joking.

After I hang up, Tammy throws her arms up and spins around. "This is awful! My friend gets stood up, and Mike—why don't you do the right thing and just get him some help?"

As though in a slow-motion replay on Film Day with Coach, I take a step toward Tammy. But as soon as I do, Shane comes up from behind and slaps me on the back.

It startles me—I'm off-balance, which leads me to fall against a student behind me—

Which makes her spit punch all over a guy—

Which makes him jump back, bumping the punch table—

Which leads the punch bowl to tip over and empty onto the assistant principal and the floor.

It takes all of three seconds—three seconds, and my life goes from bad to bad-bad-bad-bad-bad-bad-bad, which is what Zeke says each time a team scores a touchdown and extra point against us. One *bad* for each point scored. If only life had a mercy rule.

11 / MONDAY, OCTOBER 21—
HISTORY CLASS

I'm the first to arrive in class. For me, it's test day. Not a test of American history but of my recent past.

Question 1: Why did Mike stand up Cindy?

Question 2: Will Tammy ever speak to Mike again?

Question 3: Will Tammy ever speak to *me* again?

Essay question: Am I doing the right thing,

covering up Mike's condition?

Before I can answer, Rashad speaks. "How you feeling?" Like way too many others, he witnessed the Kyle-and-Tammy-and-punch-bowl homecoming havoc.

"Like Lee at Appomattox," I joke. "You got a white flag?"

"You need more than that." Rashad points at the door.

There's Tammy, staring hard. Next to her is Cindy, staring even harder.

I leave Rashad, my desk, and my books behind and join them at the door. Before I can speak, Tammy turns her back and starts to walk away. Cindy follows.

"Tammy, wait up!" I shout, but she's in speed-walk mode.

She and Cindy take a hard right into the choir room and slam the door. I open it and step inside.

The room is empty save for Cindy, Tammy, and my conscience.

"So, Kyle, do you have something you want to say to Cindy?" Tammy asks.

I step forward. "Cindy, I'm sorry about Mike. He's going through a hard time."

Tammy frowns. "Text him. Tell him where we are, and tell him to be here."

I do as she says.

Unlike all day Saturday and Sunday, Mike actually texts back. I tell him to meet me in the choir room and hit Send just as the second bell rings. "We're late for class," I say.

"This is more important," says Tammy.

I look down at the choir room carpet and throw blocks in my head as the three of us wait in silence.

"Kyle, we're late for—" Mike says as he enters, but he stops when he sees Cindy and Tammy. He shoots me a dirty look. "Wow, what a setup. Thanks."

Cindy takes a step toward Mike. Her face is beet red and her lower lip shakes. "You stood me up. You know how embarrassed I am? My mom and dad wanted to meet you." With that, the tears start to flow.

Tammy steps over and hugs her.

Mike gives me a look like *What do I do now?*

but I shrug my shoulders. He's too far downfield for me to help him on this play. He steps toward Cindy and places a hand on her shoulder. "I'm sorry. I must have had the flu or something. I fell asleep after work on Saturday. To be honest, I don't remember much until waking up for school this morning."

Tammy shakes her head and bites her lip. She knows the truth about Mike.

Mike motions for Cindy to join him at a table in a corner of the room. "Cindy, can we—?"

She follows, slowly. Once they sit, her sadness seems to fade somewhat. But when I turn to face Tammy, she's anything but smiles.

I hold out my hand. "Are we good?" I ask.

She takes it.

"I want to do what's best," I tell her, "but I don't know what that is. Don't force this on me, Tammy, please."

In the corner, Mike seems more himself until the end-of-period bell rings on the wall above him. The three of us watch as he grabs his ears as if to keep them from jumping off his skull.

12 / MONDAY, OCTOBER 21— AFTERNOON FILM REVIEW

"Kyle, you puked up worse than my old hunting dog!" Zeke announces to teammates assembled to watch game film. Zeke walked into the locker room after Mike vomited, so I told him I was the one who threw up.

"Shut up, Zeke," I say.

Mike is at my side, wiping his mouth.

"Maybe you got your brains scrambled, and the Z-Man's gonna take your minutes," Zeke shoots back. He turns his attention to Mike. "Were you in there, helping clean up your friend's vomit?"

Mike doesn't respond.

"Next time I gotta puke, I'll know who to call," Zeke continues.

I lean into Mike. "Hey, I think it's time you show Zeke who's the better wrestler, don't you?"

With that, Mike turns and heads full bore in Zeke's direction.

Zeke tries to scramble out of his chair. "Now, wait, man—" but there's nothing he can do. Mike is on him like color on a crayon, and the two fall to the floor, Zeke's head hitting the hard tile.

"Owwww!" says Zeke.

When Mike stands back up, Zeke is still on the floor, squinting.

"Good one, Mike," Devon says. "He's mouthed off too many times, if you ask me." He goes to help Zeke up, but Zeke's not moving.

"Z-Man!" Devon shouts.

Zeke moves—some—while Mike and I take our seats up front.

"Wha' happened?" asks Zeke.

There's more commotion, and when I turn back, I see Zeke sitting on the floor, holding his head with both hands while a few players stand over him.

Devon comes over to fist-bump Mike. "You rung him good, man."

Coach Whitson walks in the room to see the players huddled around Zeke. "What's going on?"

"I think Kyle's concussed," Zeke says in a weak voice as he continues to hold his head. "He lost his cookies in the locker room."

Coach Whitson stares at me, but I don't blink. "Kyle, see me after film," Coach says.

"Nice knowing you, Kyle," Zeke hisses as he takes a seat.

As I watch my blocks on-screen, I know there's no way Zeke could replace me, even if I were hurt. Each play is textbook. I put my body on the line every time.

"We have lots of game highlights, but then there's this low light," says Coach Colby. Mike is on the screen, missing his block, stumbling through his pass pattern, and having the ball on his fingertips for a second before getting hit.

"Here's your best play, Miller," Coach says.

Mike says nothing. Maybe he's asleep in the darkness. If so, he's missing the nightmare on film.

On the screen, Mike pulls himself up from the ground after a play and starts to run to the bench—the *other* team's bench.

"The way you've played this year, Miller, I sometimes think you'd be doing us a favor, playing for the other team. Maybe Athens High is recruiting."

The biggest laugh yet wakes Mike up. "What did he say?" Mike asks me.

I watch the film as Mike realizes his goof and recrosses the field.

"Nothing important," I respond.

After the footage, Coach Zachary and the rest of the staff decide to celebrate last week's victory by making us run the stadium stairs like we'd lost. I stay behind to talk to Coach Whitson.

I hadn't planned this—thanks a lot, Zeke—but it couldn't have worked out better. If Coach believes Zeke's line about me being concussed, maybe they'll give me some new concussion test. If that's the case, I'll know what to expect in case they give Mike the same test. We beat two tests, we can beat a third. Like the Troy football team, Mike and I can go undefeated if we work together.

"We need to talk," Coach Whitson begins.

He knows about Mike is all I can think. "Anything wrong?"

"It's Mike." My heart pounds louder than the band's drum line. "He's playing hard but not smart this year, and we're out of options at tight end."

"What about Norwood?" I ask.

Coach Whitson shakes his head.

"How about Steve or—"

"No, I want you to take snaps tomorrow, and I want you to start for Friday's game. Zeke can take your—"

"Why not have Zeke play tight end?" I ask. I do *not* want to be the one to take Mike's minutes.

"Zeke doesn't have all the tools you need for that position." Coach points at his forehead. "You, I trust. You're starting. We're done."

I start toward the field, wondering how I'll tell Mike the news that he's history. I have to think of something, and before I reach the first stair, the answer comes to me—*history*. Like General Grant, I can be cunning. On Tuesday, like Coach said, I could play TE but ever so subtly fail. Then on Wednesday, Zeke would play and likely fail too. By Thursday, maybe Mike will be ready to play.

But there's a catch: if I play poorly on purpose so that Mike can move up, I let the whole team down. Not only that, I risk my own dream of making it to State. If Mike's injury keeps him from playing for State, I can't blow my own chance to make it.

In history class, we learned that it was Sherman who said, "War is hell." If he was here right now, I'm sure he'd say the same about football.

13 / TUESDAY, OCTOBER 22— AFTERNOON PRACTICE

"Miller, get in there!" Whitson yells, and Mike runs onto the field.

It's a lucky break—well, lucky if you're anyone but Brian Norwood. I started at tight end just as Coach had asked and Norwood played tackle, but then Norwood pulled a hamstring. That left Coach with no other option but to put Mike back in.

I give Mike the thumbs-up and shift back

to my tackle position. Mike delivers to Shane the play Coach wants us to practice. We break huddle and line up. I'm back where I belong— on the line, with Mike by my side.

Even though we're just running plays— there's no defense—Shane yells out the signal like it's game day. Every second of every minute of every practice, coaches want us to treat it like it's real. Shane takes the snap, fakes the pitch, and drops back in the pocket. Since Mike stayed in to block, Shane's poised to throw long to Orlando or Terry, but before Shane can toss the perfect spiral, Coach Whitson blows the whistle. Everyone stops.

"What was that?" Coach yells, running over to Shane. Shane answers, repeating the play call Mike gave him. Coach pivots and stomps toward Mike. "Miller, take your helmet off!"

Mike does as he's told.

Coach Whitson leans in. "Son, do you have anything between those ears?! That's not the play I called!"

Mike hangs his head as Coach keeps yelling. "You can't catch, can't block—you can't even bring in the right plays!" Coach's face is a lovely shade of crimson. "Just what *can* you do, Miller?"

More silence from Mike. I hear a few guys laugh.

"Who finds this funny?" Coach shouts. He takes a step toward Zeke. "Was that you laughing, Mr. Muller? You haven't had your head in the game since August!"

Coach takes another step toward Devon. "And Mr. Shaw, you dropped the ball twice today—and there isn't any defense on the field!" Coach gathers himself. "Guys, you're the best this school's got, but you have to pull it together."

Coach turns his attention to Mike again. "So when I say forward rush, twenty-one, that's the play you deliver to, alright?"

Coach Whitson blows his whistle loud, right in front of Mike. "Same play again," he says.

I remove my helmet and follow Coach to the sideline while I glance at Mike. I know that if our fates are connected, Mike would do the same for me.

"Coach," I say, "I'll help Mike get it together. We're not gonna let you down. Remember, Mike and I are headed to State—"

Coach turns to me quickly and interrupts, "I know, I know, that 'shared dream' thing, right? If you guys are so close, help him put his head in the game. Calling the wrong play? A mistake like that could cost us a victory. Now get back in the lineup."

"Yes, sir!" I say.

As I sprint back to the line of scrimmage, it dawns on me: I'm covering for Mike to save myself. I have no other goals or dreams. I've invested everything—blood, heart, soul—into the Mike-and-Kyle-football-hero story. If that dream fails, there's no backup plan, nothing. On the field, I protect the quarterback. Off the field, I guard the shared dream of Mike and me.

On Shane's signal, we run the play. It's picture perfect. We run it five more times and then switch to a pass play that we run ten times. I look at everyone on the team. No one speaks. Everyone's focused. Coach's rant did the trick.

At the end of practice, Coach is so pleased that he tells us all to take the stairs. "Ten sets, everyone."

Mike joins me at the base of the stairs. "What did you say to Coach?" he asks.

"Nothing important." We run the stairs, but at least we run them together.

14 / WEDNESDAY, OCTOBER 23— LATE EVENING

Brang-a-la-la—

I'm in the huddle. Tom Brady eyes me, "You got this, Kyle," he says.

Brang-a-la-la, brang-a-la-la—

The huddle breaks. The line forms.

Brang-a-la-la—

My eyes open. It's my phone on the head-board. I reach up to shut it off when I realize it's not my alarm, it's a call.

I read the screen.

11:47 p.m.
INCOMING CALL
Mike Miller

"Yo," I answer.

"You busy?"

I stretch in bed. "Busy? Almost midnight on a school night, you kidding? I'm on my way to the mall for some hair care products, actually."

"I bet I woke you. It's me, Mike."

"Don't worry about it. I was just dreaming that one of the finest quarterbacks to ever play the game was gonna hand off to me, but that's OK. What's up?"

"I can't do this anymore. I gotta get help."

"Two weeks, Mike. Two weeks, remember?"

There's a pause. "What about two weeks?" he asks.

I pull myself up and rest on my elbow. I had explained this to him already. "It was on the website we visited, don't you remember? It said take it easy for two weeks after a concussion."

"Oh, yeah," Mike says, but just as quickly, he continues, "Kyle, my memory hasn't been that good. I don't remember what it said."

I remind him of the high points of the article but leave out the finer details. Like the detail that you should always seek medical attention immediately after a concussion. Like the detail that said there should be no contact sports until you're cleared to play by a medical professional. And the detail that two weeks is the average time someone should rest, but more severe concussions may require more time.

"How long has it been?" Mike asks.

"Has what been?"

"Since I got hit. It must be two weeks. How many games have we played since?"

"It's been almost two weeks."

There's silence on the other end, as though the call dropped.

"You still there?" I ramp up the concern in my voice.

"I'm still here. Gus sent me home again. He's not gonna take much more of me. I did my best, Kyle, it's just, I couldn't remember—"

I can tell from his voice he's crying.

I turn the light on next to my bed. "Here's the new plan. Are you listening?"

"I'm listening."

"There's just one more game, one more, and that's it. If you don't feel better after Friday's game, we'll go to Dr.—what's his face?—Nussbaum. We'll go to him together and tell him everything, OK?"

"OK."

"Friday. One more game. Hang in there, OK?"

"OK."

We talk for a few more minutes, then end the call. I turn the light out, lay back down, close my eyes, and hope Tom Brady hasn't forgotten the play.

15 / THURSDAY, OCTOBER 24—
LUNCH HOUR

"So, we're breaking up over this?" Tammy asks. We're in her car. I'm hungry, but that's not what's eating away at my stomach. "I can't believe it, Kyle."

"I'm sorry, Tammy, but you're not giving me a choice." Truth is she did give me a choice when she told me to either tell the coaches about Mike or tell her good-bye. "He's my friend. We've got a plan. I need to help him."

"But you're not helping him!" Her yelling is too loud for such a small space. I hate her stupid Honda.

"Look, he's gonna get one last chance to start, I know it. Zeke's hopeless. Brian refuses to play TE. So it's Mike or give away the running and short-pass game."

"How is that helping him? If he's hurt, he could only get hurt worse. Why don't you—"

"I don't want to talk about it!"

"Kyle, you're smarter than that," Tammy says. "I understand you don't want to snitch on a friend, but maybe you could confide in one of the coaches. Mike would never have to find out. What about that?"

I laugh. "You don't get it."

"Don't get what?"

I tell her the harsh truth about Troy football. "If they think Mike can help us win, they won't care if his back is broken. They'd tape him up and send him to the line."

"What if he got hurt on the field?"

"They'd just find more tape. All the coaches care about is winning. At all costs."

Tammy starts to argue, but I remind her of the various antics of the Big Six starting backs and the way Coach Z ignores them, and she knows I speak the truth.

"I don't know how you can stand it," she says.

I reach my hand toward her, but she doesn't take it. "Because of the dream, Tammy."

"The dream?"

"The dream Mike and I have had since probably the first time we put on shoulder pads." My mind flashes back to game after game, the two of us side by side. "We've dreamed of going to OSU together."

Tammy reaches across the car and touches my forehead. "Wake up, Kyle. Wake up."

"No, we're going to do it," I push her hand—weighed down with my senior ring—away.

Tammy shakes her head. "I don't know what else to say. You trusted me when you told me about Mike, and I trusted that, when the time came, you'd do the right thing. But you won't do it."

"Why can't you support me on this?" I sound like a toddler, begging for a toy. "He's my friend. I helped your friend Cindy out, got her invited to homecoming. Sure, Mike stood—"

"You've lost touch with reality," Tammy says, her tone cold like a stranger. "Let me tell you what the reality is. Mike is hurt. If he keeps playing, he risks getting hurt even worse. You're not helping, Kyle. If he's your friend and you care about him—and you care about me—then you'll do the right thing."

I put my head in my hands and mumble, "No."

Without saying a word, she holds out a closed fist and nods. She drops my senior ring into my palm and unlocks the door. "Go," she says.

I step out into the parking lot at the same moment a cold, October wind blows.

Do the right thing, she said. Like I know what that is. It's fourth and twenty, and Tammy just gave me a two-minute warning.

16 / THURSDAY, OCTOBER 24—
BEFORE FOOTBALL PRACTICE

I hustle from my locker to the locker room, but it's no good—I'll be ten minutes late for practice no matter what I do. I hear Coach's voice in my head: *Ten minutes late, Kyle. Ten laps around the field.* Just once—just *once*—I'd like him to reward bad behavior. *Ten minutes late for practice, Kyle? Hope we didn't inconvenience you. Here's $10. Go buy yourself a pizza.*

Shane bounds around the corner from the

hallway next to the gym. "It's not good, man, not good."

Not good? A million things cross my mind, each with one thing in common—Mike.

"What's wrong?" I ask.

"They say he has a concussion. But we totally need him against Dayton Bluff."

My heart sinks. I look down the hallway. There's no one in sight. "What do you mean, they pulled him?"

"There's a different concussion doc in the lockers, and this guy is super thorough. I mean, he checks everything, like I had to walk and do this thing with my fingers . . . This guy is good."

"So they pulled Mike?" I asked.

"Mike?" Shane pauses. "What makes you say that?"

Now I'm in trouble. "No reason. I just—"

"It's Z-Man," says Shane. "He's concussed, and they think it might have happened Monday when he and Mike got into it."

I quicken my pace toward the lockers. A new doctor. One day before our next home game. I didn't see this coming at all. Mike and

I have beaten every test so far, but this one sounds big.

As I near the lockers, Coach Zachary sees me and immediately looks at his watch. "Twelve minutes late for practice, Kyle," he says.

"I know, I know. Twelve laps, right?"

Coach laughs. "Only if you want to. I'm starting practice a half hour late. We've got another concussion doctor here with us."

About twenty players are seated inside the locker room, but I don't see a doctor—or Mike.

Zeke's seated on a bench nearby.

"Hey, did I hear right?" I ask.

"Yeah, benched for two weeks," he says, picking at a fingernail.

"Sorry about that, man. Take care of yourself, right? You might need that brain later on." I look around the room. "Where's this new doctor?"

Zeke points to a room inside the lockers. "In there."

"You've seen Mike?" I ask.

"He's in there with him," says Zeke.

I almost collapse on the bench. If I had been

tested before Mike, I maybe could've coached him on what to expect. I look at the door and imagine what's going on in the room.

The door bursts open and a tall man in a lab coat rushes out. He shouts into his phone as he rushes to the hall. "Possibly two weeks post status. If Dr. Henry's available, I'll need an eval ASAP—"

When the man reaches the hall, he holds the phone to his chest and shouts, "Coach! Coach!"

From off in the distance, Coach Z responds. "Yes, sir?"

The man in the lab coat is frantic. "I need a second ambulance, and someone should go out front and wave them in. This boy needs help immediately."

Zeke and I watch everything unfold. Under his breath, Zeke whispers, "Dang."

Coach rushes into the locker, and the two men stand outside the door, looking at Mike.

"There's hemorrhaging. He says he's had it almost two weeks. I've ordered an eval for an ICP—"

Coach stops him. "ICP?"

The doc turns. "Intracranial pressure monitor. His brain is bleeding. It's causing pressure in his head."

Through the two of them, I can see Mike in the room, facing the door. His body is limp, but his face says it all—relief.

17 / FRIDAY, OCTOBER 25—
HOME GAME AGAINST DAYTON BLUFF
BULLDOGS

"Offside. Troy. Number 60."

The refs in high school football don't have mics like they do in the NFL, but it doesn't matter. Everybody saw me jump. Everybody knows I'm guilty. I've taken as many penalties in this game—two—as I've taken the rest of my probably-over-and-done-with high school football career.

"Head in the game!" Coach Zachary shouts from the sidelines. People in the stands yell just as loud. I jog back to the huddle and wait for Shane to tear me a new one.

But he doesn't. He takes the play from Brian—back at tight end, against his wishes—and lines us up, preparing to pass. Because of my mistake, it's now third and nine. Shane's toss goes long, which he loves—any chance he can get to show off his golden arm.

My Bulldog opponent isn't stronger, smarter, or more skilled than me, but he's playing dirty. On every down, he slams his helmet hard into mine. He does it so fast, the refs don't see, but I don't say anything. I don't complain because I deserve it.

Shane takes the snap and drops back. We close the pocket around him while he looks for an open receiver. The crowd's cheering, but my ears are ringing. The dirty Bulldog blasts his helmet into mine.

The pass falls short—just as I fell short as a lineman, a teammate, and a friend.

Shane and the rest of the Big Six head for

the sidelines as the punt squad takes the field.

At the snap, I bulldoze my Bulldog foe with pent-up rage—not at him but at myself. The punt sails high through the night sky, a thing of beauty in the ugly world of high school football.

At halftime, Coach Zachary tries to inspire us, while Colby calls us ladies and Whitson asks when we're going to man up. I hear about every other word because my ears are still ringing. I stare at Mike's empty locker, but all I see are images of him in a hospital bed. I close my eyes and think about another set of lockers, the ones at OSU with our names on them. My eyes shut tighter, not just to block the harsh lights of the locker room, but to hold back tears, to hold onto the fading dream.

"You want to rack up another loss this season?" Coach Zachary shouts. "You really want to lose in front of your friends and family? There is no tomorrow. This is it. Everything in your life that matters comes down to the next twenty-four minutes. Understand?"

There's a lot of head shaking and shouting. If Mike was here, he'd probably be the loudest.

"Let's go!" Colby shouts.

Everyone heads for the locker room door, ready to burst out of the tunnel and win another game for the pride of Troy and the ego of Coach Zachary. I hold my helmet in my hand, frozen on the bench.

"Kyle, let's go!" Coach Whitson shouts.

"I'm hurt," I whisper. "I think I have a concussion."

He stands over me, puts his hand on my shoulder and says, "It can wait."

"Wait?" I ask.

He leans close to me, his mouth almost on my ear. "We need you to win. Get out there."

———————————

"What are you doing here?" Tammy asks when I find her in the stands at the start of the fourth quarter.

After I handed Coach Whitson my jersey, I walked around the parking lot for a long time. I texted Mike, but he didn't pick up.

"I quit." I tell Tammy everything. Cindy, seated next to her, hears it all too.

Tammy puts her hand in mine. My knuckles are the colors of Christmas: green from the turf, red from blood. "It's OK, Kyle," she says.

"It's not, though. None of it. It's not OK how I covered up."

"You thought you were doing the right thing," Cindy says. Like everyone else, all she knows is that Mike's in the hospital, but coaches told the team not to speak out about why. They didn't tell us to win the game for Mike or Zeke. The coaches want to pretend as though nothing ever happened.

As I'm not on the team anymore, I tell her about Mike's concussion, about Nussbaum's concussion program, and how I helped Mike beat the tests.

"I feel terrible about some of the things I said to Mike," Cindy says.

"You didn't know. It's not your fault," I say.

"Kyle, it's not *your* fault," Tammy whispers. I doubt she believes it, but it's nice of her to say.

I reach into my pocket and hand her back my class ring. She takes it.

"I should have listened to you," I say.

She kisses me gently on my hurting forehead and puts the ring on her finger. I won't wear a state championship ring at the end of this season. I won't have a locker at OSU nor will Mike. Those were good dreams, but in dreams lay choices, even the choice to drop the dream.

18 / SATURDAY, OCTOBER 26—
TROY GENERAL HOSPITAL

It's my first text of the day: *Library today?*

Morn babe, I text back.

Morn library today?

And hospital.

CU @ 10

Tammy and I make it to the library, where I spend two hours of intense studying—of her hands, her hair, and Sherman's march to Atlanta—before making our way to the hospital to see Mike.

"Here's something," I whisper.

Tammy looks up from a small stack of books.

"The Sherman tank? They named it after the guy we've been studying, William Tecumseh Sherman."

"Neat fact. Find a place for it in the presentation," Tammy whispers back.

"I want a tank named after *me*," I say. "When I cut through an offensive line, lay waste a field of—"

"Your tank days are over. You don't play football anymore," Tammy reminds me. "No more tackling."

I drop my pencil. She's right. Dropping football dropped so much of what I was. Like Atlanta after Sherman's destructive march, everything going forward will be focused on rebuilding.

Once inside the hospital, Tammy and I stop at the information desk and learn that Mike is on the third floor.

We take the elevator. As I step into the

hallway, my legs feel heavy. What shape will Mike be in? Is he upset? And if he is upset, is he upset with himself or me?

Tammy and I walk slowly toward the room. I lean against her arm for support. A few steps from the door, I hear my name: "Kyle?"

It's Mike's dad—the father of the guy I helped put in the hospital. I think about running but, instead, stand to take whatever blow I have coming.

"So good to see you," he says as he grabs my arm to shake my hand.

So even Mike's dad doesn't know I helped Mike cover up his injury.

"Hello, Mr. Miller."

"And what a beautiful lady you've brought with you," he says.

Tammy sticks her hand out. "I'm Tammy. Mike and I have a history class together."

"Mike's asleep, which they tell me is good for him—he needs rest. Follow me. There's a waiting room down the hall."

Mike and his dad have the same build—tall as a barn and about as wide—only Mike's dad has this thick white beard that makes him look like Santa Claus on steroids.

Inside the waiting room, Mike's mom puts down her magazine and rushes to greet me. "Kyle!" she says. She gives me a quick hug and a kiss on the cheek.

For the second time in a week, I'm an inch tall.

"Mike would be so happy to see you," says Mrs. Miller. She wears a Walmart uniform and a smile as wide as goalposts.

I introduce her to Tammy, and the four of us sit.

"You and Mike go back to midget league, right?" asks Mr. Miller.

"Yes, sir," I say. Mike's folks work so much, I rarely see them.

Mrs. Miller chimes in. "You and he are such good friends. Mike talks about you all the time."

The conversation goes on like this for a few minutes, seesawing between stories from the midget league days to the here and now.

"The doctor is hopeful," says Mr. Miller. "Besides," he says, reaching for his wife's hand, "whatever we need to do, we'll do it. Mike's our only son, you know?"

"Yes, I know," I say. On life's ruler, I now stand a half inch tall, given all that I could have done for Mike but chose not to.

"But there is one thing," Mrs. Miller adds, her voice as serious as Coach Z explaining a new play. "I hope this doesn't upset you, but the doctor says he should never play football again. You'll have to play for State without him."

On the ruler, I don't even register.

19 / MONDAY, OCTOBER 28—
FILM DAY

Outside the classroom, I can hear the voices of my former teammates. It takes all of my strength to go and see them, but I have to. Coach called me to the meeting himself.

No one has seen me yet, so I stand outside the room to listen.

"OK, brutes, grab a seat," says Coach. "Friday night was a bust. We lost the game, and we lost three good players, all seniors. Two to this concussion-brain thing and a third to, well, you'll have to ask him why. But even with a loss, we're still on track to make the playoffs."

There's howling from inside the room, which stops as quickly as it starts.

"Which means that we can't lose focus before we travel to Bradbury for Friday's game against the Cyclones."

The chorus of boos from inside the room is loud enough to vibrate the floor.

"Practices are gonna be hard this week, boys and girls. There's no denying it. No way we're letting you get soft before it's time to play Athens—"

At that moment, Nussbaum exits the room and spies me. His eyes widen as he points at me, "You're the boy."

I have no idea what's he's talking about, but it doesn't matter. He quickly goes back into the room and returns with Coach Z.

"Kyle," says Coach. "I didn't think you had it in you to show your face to the team, and I was right."

"Well, I—"

"Never mind," says Coach. He turns to ask another coach to take over for him, then returns to me. "Follow me."

I do as he says and follow him to his office. Nussbaum follows me all the while, close enough that if I put on the brakes, I'd flatten him. I choose to play nice instead and keep the pace with Coach.

In the office, I take a seat in front of Coach's desk while Nussbaum takes the other chair.

Coach reaches into a drawer, pulls out a toothpick, and begins to chew. "You know, Kyle," he begins, "the school board frowns upon ambulances pulling up to its properties, especially when it's a—"

"Grade three concussion, hemorrhage," Nussbaum says.

The toothpick spirals in Coach's mouth. "Now, you've said before how close you two are." He pulls the toothpick out and points it at me like a weak sword. "I have to ask, did you know anything about this?"

I adjust myself in the chair. What's done is done, I think to myself. I can tell the truth, but

I don't have to tell everything. "Yes, I knew he was having headaches. He said that's why he wore sunglasses—it helped him. But I had no idea how bad it was."

Nussbaum flips. He leans forward, exasperated. "No idea?"

I look in Nussbaum's face full-on. "No, doctor. That was your job," I say.

"Kyle," says Coach with a stern face, "we've all got our job to do, and Dr. Nussbaum here did what he could—"

"No, he didn't." I turn to Dr. Nussbaum, "Sure, we had tests, but they were easy to beat."

Dr. Nussbaum leans back in his chair. "What do you mean?" he asks.

For the next ten minutes, I explain everything. How we beat the eye exam by saying Mike had a head cold, how the nurse left the exams unattended in the room. I explain Mike's sunglasses and all the plays Mike missed—that each was a sign that something was wrong. "You thought Mike didn't have his head in the game. Did you ever think it might have been something bigger?"

The two men are silent for a moment.

"As for why I quit, Coach—in the game against Dayton Bluffs, the defensive back knocked my helmet every chance he could. At the half, I was about ready to throw up, and then Whitson told me to get back out there and win the game. I saw what happened to Mike," I add. "I didn't want it to happen to me."

Coach flicks his toothpick up and down.

Nussbaum flattens his hands on his knees. "I needed this," he says. "I knew we'd have to make changes to the program, but I didn't think they'd come so soon."

With that, Nussbaum stood, shakes Coach's hand, then turns to me and says, "I'm sorry for Mike, but you have no idea how many young people you may have helped today. If you'll excuse me, I've got a lot of work to do."

As he leaves, I can hear him murmuring, "Train all coaching staff. Laptops for the tests. We can do the testing online with real-time feedback . . ."

With Nussbaum out of the room, it's just Coach and me. "Kyle, thanks for what you did here. I wish I could have you back, what with the Bradbury game this week, but you made your decision."

"Thanks for all the good memories," I say. Then Coach and I shake hands.

I leave the office and walk down the hall to the exit. Once there, I open the door, knowing I've cut every string holding me to football. My equipment—helmet, pads, tapes—only weighed a few pounds, but I feel much lighter, more like a feather than a cannonball.

ABOUT THE AUTHORS

Patrick Jones is the author of more than twenty books for teen readers, including works with a focus on contact sports such as mixed martial arts (The Dojo series), boxing (*The Gamble*), and football (*Out of the Tunnel*). A former librarian for teenagers, Jones won lifetime achievement awards in 2006 from the American Library Association and Catholic Library Association. As a Michigan native and current resident of Minnesota, he's locked into the power battles of the NFC Central, but for him, pro football hasn't been the same since the original Cleveland Browns left Ohio in 1995.

Brent Chartier served as a magazine editor for ten years. *At All Costs* is his second book for young readers. His interest in concussions stems from his work with the Center for Neurological Studies, Dearborn, Michigan. He lives in a Detroit suburb with his son, Casey, and their cat.

THE **RED** ZONE

WINNING IS *NOT OPTIONAL.*